"Can we read it?"
"Yes we can!"

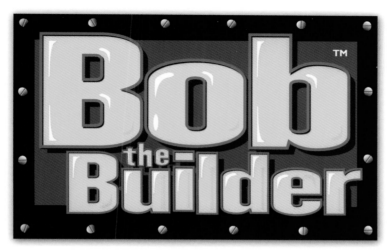

Story Treasury

EGMONT

We bring stories to life

First published in Great Britain in 2007 by Egmont UK Limited,
239 Kensington High Street, London W8 6SA
Edited by Brenda Apsley and designed by Jeannette O'Toole

HiT entertainment

ISBN 978 1 4052 3472 6
1 3 5 7 9 10 8 6 4 2
Printed in U.A.E.

This
Bob the Builder
Story Treasury
belongs to

....

....

"The fun is in getting it done!"

Story Treasury

a special collection of
Bob the Builder stories

EGMONT

Contents

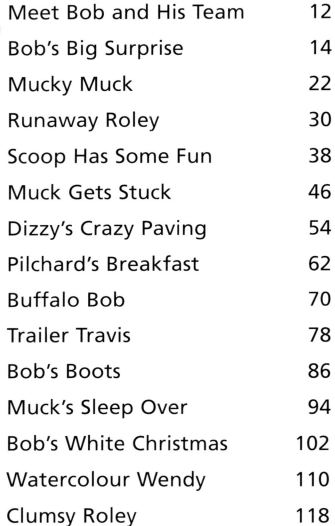

Meet Bob and His Team

Bob learned all about building from his dad, **Robert**.

They built the **Bobsville** house and yard together.

When Bob needed help **Wendy** became his partner.

Scoop, the big digger, joined the team.

Then Bob got a digger-dumper called **Muck**.

Next came **Dizzy** the cement mixer,

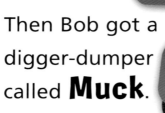

and **Lofty** the mobile crane.

Roley the steamroller came with his friend **Bird**.

Bob's cat **Pilchard** is part of the team, too!

Farmer Pickles has a farm near Bobsville. Bob helps him and he helps Bob!

The farm puppy is called **Scruffty**.

Spud the scarecrow scares crows like **Squawk**.

Travis is the farm tractor.

Bob buys things he needs from **JJ**'s yard.

JJ's daughter **Molly** helps him.

The delivery truck is called **Skip** and

Trix is the forklift truck!

Wendy is my partner
in the building yard. She's
a great builder! When she
went on holiday we made
a surprise for her. But my
cat, Pilchard, gave me
a surprise, too!
Read about how
Wendy got a new
garden in . . .

Bob's Big Surprise

Wendy was going to see her sister's new garden.

"Mrs Potts will look after the office," she told Bob.

Scoop took Wendy to the station.

"I'll miss Wendy," said Dizzy.

"So will I," said Bob. "But we'll be busy while she's away. We're going to make her a new garden!"

Next morning, Mrs Potts rang Bob. She was ill, so she couldn't work in the office.

Bob told the others the news. "Don't worry," he said. "We'll manage. Let's get to work!"

"Can we fix it?" said Scoop.

"Yes we can!" said the others.

All except Lofty. "Er . . . yeah . . . I think so," he said.

Scoop and Roley went to pick up the new grass.

Bob, Muck, Dizzy and Lofty went to Wendy's garden.

"We're going to build a patio and a pergola," Bob told them.

Muck rolled the ground flat for the patio. Dizzy mixed some mortar. Lofty carried wood. Bob then made the pergola.

"Er, what's a pergola, Bob?" asked Lofty.

Bob explained. "It's a place to sit in, made of wood."

At the yard, Pilchard was trying to sleep. But the phone rang, **brrrrrring!** and the answering machine said, "Please leave a message after the beep. **Beeeeep!**"

"Waaaaaoooh!" said Pilchard. When the phone rang again, **brrrrrring!** she hit it with her paw!

When Bob came back to the office, he found there were no messages. The machine just said **gabble-gabble-gabble.**

"Oh, well," said Bob, and he went back to the garden.

When Scoop and Roley arrived with the grass, Wendy's garden was ready.

Pilchard was fast asleep. Then the phone rang again, **brrrrrring-brrrrrring!** The answering machine said, **"Ples leve a mesagegefthny . . . "**

"Waaarrrohh!" said Pilchard, angrily.

When Bob came back to the office he got a surprise! The phone was off the hook and the answering machine was broken. Naughty Pilchard!

Bob went back to the garden again.

"Surprise!" he said when Wendy came home.

"It's lovely!" said Wendy. "Thank you!"

Later on, Wendy asked, "How was Mrs Potts?"

"She was ill," said Bob. "The office is a bit of a mess."

"I'll sort it out," said Wendy. "Then I'll enjoy my lovely new garden. What about adding a fountain?"

Poor Bob! He didn't say a word!

When Travis the tractor
got stuck in the mud, Muck
pulled him out. But Muck
didn't like what came next!
Read about Wendy and
Farmer Pickles'
surprise in . . .

Mucky Muck

It rained hard all day! When Bob, Scoop and Muck got back to the yard they were covered in sticky mud.

"I'll wash you when the rain stops," Bob told them.

Muck didn't like the sound of that! He loves being dirty!

"Did Bob say **wash?**" he said to Scoop. "Oh, no!"

Spud didn't like the rain. He sat under the cover in Travis' trailer until it stopped.

"You can come out now," said Travis. "I have to get back to the farm."

But the rain had made the ground very muddy. When Travis tried to move, his wheels just spun round and round.

"I'm stuck!" he said.

Farmer Pickles told Bob about Travis getting stuck in the mud.

"Muck will get him out," said Bob. "His special tracks won't get stuck."

Muck was pleased. Now he could stay mucky and messy!

"Can I help, Bob?" asked Dizzy.

"Yes," said Bob. "You can carry the rope."

Bob tied one end of the rope to Travis. He tied the other end to Muck.

"Can you tow it?" said Bob.

"Yes I . . . uh . . . oof . . . can!" said Muck.

He pulled and pulled until – **shlup!** – Travis came flying out of the mud. It went all over Muck!

"You're even muckier now, Muck!" said Dizzy.

"I know!" said Muck. "Mucky Muck, that's me! Great!"

Spud threw messy mud pies at Muck and Dizzy. "Got you!" he laughed.

Muck scooped up mud in his digger. He threw it at Spud. "Take that!" he said.

Bob laughed. "Stop that and come up to the farmyard," he told them. "Farmer Pickles has a surprise for you!"

Bob told Muck, Dizzy and Spud to stand in a line. "Now close your eyes," he said. "No peeping!"

They couldn't see Farmer Pickles and Wendy coming with big buckets of soapy water!

Bob started to wash Muck. Poor Muck didn't like it at all. "Not fun! Not fun!" he said.

"It's only a bit of water, Muck!" said Spud.

"That's right," said Farmer Pickles. "And it's your turn next, Spud."

"WHAT?" said Spud. **"ME? WATER? SOAP?** No way! I'm off! See you later!"

One night, Roley fell asleep as soon as he got back to the yard. When he set off again the next morning, he was still fast asleep! Read about what happened to him in . . .

Runaway Roley

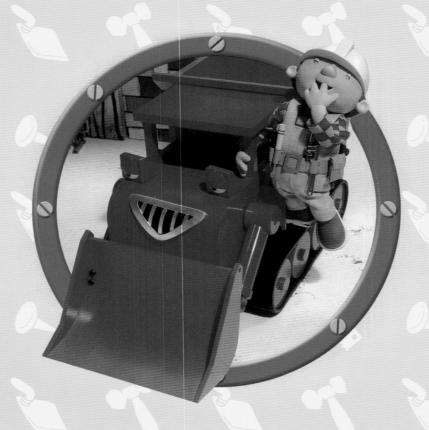

Bob, Roley and Muck worked very hard all day. They were really tired when they got back to the yard.

Bob yawned. "It's been a long day," he said.

Roley closed his eyes. "The longest ever," he said, and fell fast asleep, **zzzzzzzz!**

Very early the next morning, Roley rolled out of the yard, but he was still fast asleep!

"Miaow!" said Pilchard. She tried to tell the others, but no one took any notice.

Sleeping Roley rumbled past Farmer Pickles' farm.

Travis the tractor said, "Hello, Roley!"

But Roley didn't reply. He was still fast asleep!

"I think Roley's sleep rolling!" said Travis.

Back at the yard, Bob said, "Where's Roley?"

Bird landed on Scoop. **"Tweet! Tweet!"** said Bird.

"Bird says he's sleep walking!" said Scoop.

"Oh, no! We have to find him!" said Bob.

"Can we stop him?" said Scoop.

"Yes we can!" said the others.

"Er . . . yeah . . . I think so," said Lofty.

"We've got to wake Roley!" said Bob.

"No," said Wendy. "It might scare him. Just bring him back here to the yard to wake up when he's ready."

"Right," said Bob.

"Can we fix it?" said Scoop.

"Yes we can!"

"Er . . . yeah . . . I think so," said Lofty.

Sleeping Roley rumbled along.
He bumped into lamp posts and
knocked over bins.

"There he is!" said Scoop.

"Oh, no!" said Bob. "He's near
that big hole! If he falls in we'll
never get him out again."

Bob put a big road sign over the hole. It made a little
bridge for Roley!

Bob fixed Lofty's hook to Roley, who took him back to the
yard, still fast asleep.

When he got there, Roley woke up. "I had a really good sleep," he said. "Right, let's get going."

But now Muck was asleep. So was Dizzy. And Lofty. Roley turned to Bob. **"Can we fix it?"**

"No we can't!" said Bob. "We're all tired. We need a sleep. See you tomorrow."

Poor Roley was puzzled. "I just can't understand it!" he said.

Spud thinks playing tricks on people is great fun! But he didn't think it was very funny when Bob played a trick on him! Read all about it in . . .

Scoop Has Some Fun

The office at the yard was in a bit of a mess!

Bob and the team were working at Farmer Pickles' farm.

Wendy decided to tidy things up while they were away.

She found some of Bob's old work clothes. Then she put them into a bag to take to the recycling centre.

Scoop had a rest. Spud said, "Let's have some fun, Scoop! Let's mess about and play tricks on people!"

He put a bale of hay on Scoop's scoop and sat on it.

"Hide behind the shed, Scoop," said Spud. "Now lift me up into the air."

Scoop lifted Spud to the top of the shed! It looked as if he was in mid air! "Look, Travis!" said Spud. "Magic!"

Travis didn't know that Scoop was lifting Spud up!

Next, Scoop lifted Spud on to the barn roof. **"Wooooo!"** said Spud. "I am the voice of the sky! **Woo-wooo!"**

Muck didn't see Spud. But he heard him. "Oo-er, a ghost!" he said. "I'm going back to the yard!"

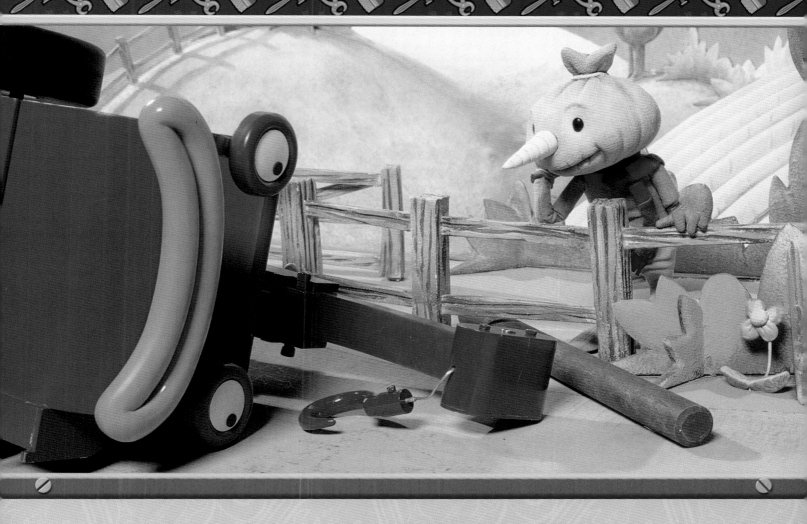

Spud played a trick on Lofty. **"Waaaaagh!"** he said, jumping out in front of him.

But Lofty was so surprised that he crashed into a big pole. It got stuck under his wheels and he fell over.

"I'm stuck!" he cried.

Spud asked Scoop to help Lofty. But Scoop thought it was another trick.

"He really is stuck," Spud told Bob. "It's true. Honest."

Bob and Scoop rescued Lofty.

It was late when they finished their jobs at the farm.

"Spud's tricks held us up a bit," said Bob.

"Yes," said Scoop. "Some of his tricks aren't very funny, are

they? I bet Spud doesn't like people playing tricks on him."

That gave Bob an idea . . .

Later on, Travis told Spud that Farmer Pickles had a new scarecrow.

Spud rushed over to him. **"Oi!"** he said. "Clear off! This is my job!"

The scarecrow put his thumbs in his ears and waggled his fingers. Spud realised that it was Bob, in his old clothes!

"Not funny!" said Spud.

"But you like tricks!" said Scoop.

"Not that one," said Spud. "But you know, you make a really good scarecrow, Bob!"

Muck doesn't like being in the dark. That's why he didn't want to go into a big black tunnel we were working on. Read about his scary day in . . .

Muck Gets Stuck

"Where are we working today, Wendy?" asked Bob.

"In the tunnel," said Wendy. "Take the generator to work the lights."

"Can we fix it?" said Scoop.

"Yes we can!" said the others.

"Er . . . yeah . . . I think so," said Lofty.

Bob asked Muck to take some bricks into the tunnel.

"But it's all . . . d-dark . . . and b-black in there," said Muck.

"I can fix that!" said Bob. "I'll use the generator to work the lights."

"Scared! Muck's scared!" said Scoop.

"I am not!" said Muck – and he sped inside the tunnel.

The generator **clanked** and **coughed** and **wheezed**. Then it stopped working and the lights went off!

"Noooooo!" said Muck. "It's too dark!"

Scoop looked in the tunnel. "Will Muck be all right?" he said. "He really is scared of the dark. Very scared."

Bob ran inside. "Follow me, Muck," he said. "You'll be all right. I've got a torch."

"I can't," said Muck. "It's too dark!"

Bob went back outside. "Muck's stuck," he said to Lofty.

Lofty went into the tunnel. "Don't worry," he said. "Come with me, Muck."

But Muck didn't move. "It's too dark," he said. "I don't like it. I can't do it."

Lofty came out. "Muck really is stuck," he told Bob.

They didn't see Pilchard go into the tunnel . . .

"**Raaaoooww!**" said Pilchard. "**RAAAOOOWW!**"

"**Acaarrgh!**" said Muck. "A g-g-ghost!"

He rushed straight out of the tunnel.

"I thought you were really stuck, Muck," said Bob.

"So did I!" said Muck.

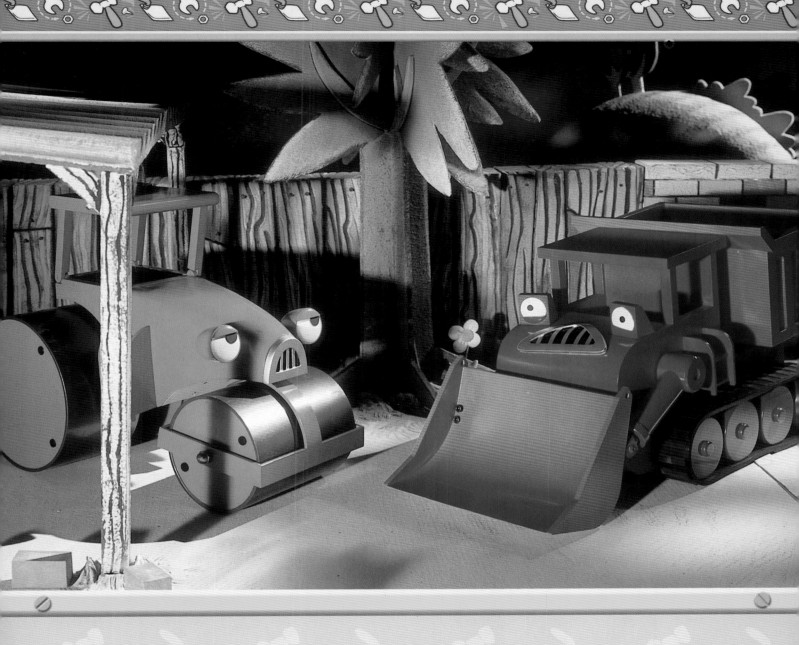

That night, Muck talked to Roley. "There was a **whooo!**
then a **clank!** That was the ghost!" he said.

"Oh, were you scared?" said Roley.

"Nah," said Muck. "Not me."

"Oh, you **are** brave!" said Roley.

When the paving
stones for Mrs Potts' new
garden path got broken,
Wendy didn't know what
to do. But Dizzy did!
Read about her bright
idea in . . .

Dizzy's Crazy Paving

Wendy and the team were making a new path in Mrs Potts' garden.

Muck carried the paving stones. "They're heavy," he said.

"So are these bags of concrete," said Dizzy.

Roley didn't have anything to carry. "But my big rollers are very heavy," he said. "I have to take them with me wherever I go."

"Can we pave it?" said Wendy.

"Yes we can!" said the others.

Wendy marked out where the path would go. Muck dumped sand on it. Roley then started to roll it flat.

"Stop, stop!" said Mrs Potts. "Roley is too big! He might break Cheeky Charlie, my favourite gnome! Please use the small hand roller, Wendy."

Roley was upset. "A little hand roller!" he said. "That won't flatten anything!"

"And it's hard work pushing it," said Wendy. **"Phew!"**

Wendy rolled the path flat. She then asked Muck to lay the stones on the path.

Roley took Wendy to where Bob was working.

Wendy helped Bob mend Mrs Broadbent's wall.

While she was away, Muck and Dizzy raced round and round Mrs Potts' garden.

Snap! Muck knocked off the end of Cheeky Charlie's nose.

Crack! The paving stones fell out of his scoop and broke into little pieces.

Wendy came back and gasped in horror. "Now what are we going to do?" she said.

"I know!" said Dizzy. "We'll use broken stones to make the path."

"Crazy paving!" said Wendy.

"Crazy Dizzy, you mean," said Muck.

"No, Dizzy's right," said Wendy. "Crazy paving is made of broken stones."

Muck and Dizzy worked hard. Muck put the pieces of stone on the path. Dizzy mixed cement to fix them in place.

Mrs Potts was pleased with her new path. "But Cheeky Charlie looks different," she said.

"Er, it's because he's near the new path," said Wendy. "He looks, er, cheekier than ever!"

"The path **is** lovely," said Mrs Potts.

"I got the idea when Muck dropped the . . . " said Dizzy.

"Er . . . Dizzy means it was a **smashing** idea!" said Wendy.

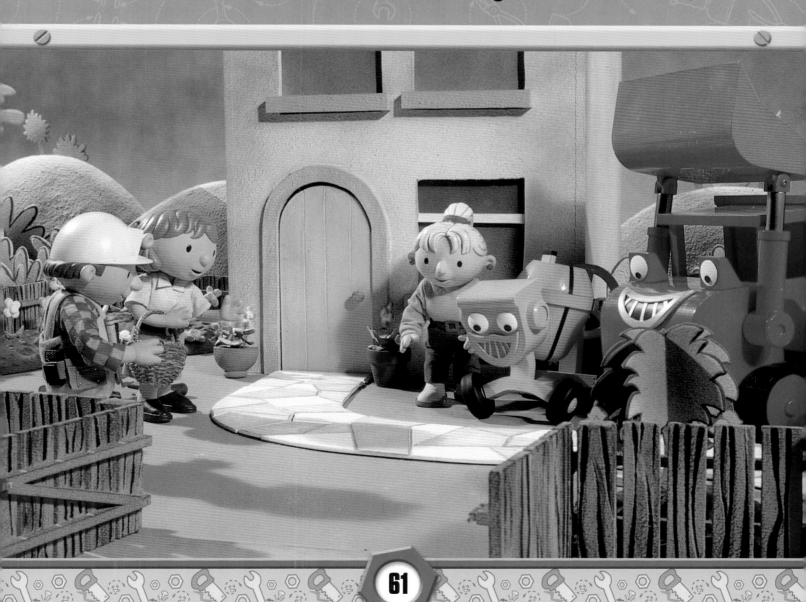

My cat, Pilchard, loves watching television, sleeping – and eating! Read about what happened one day, when I forgot all about feeding her in . . .

Pilchard's Breakfast

"Morning everyone!" said Bob.

Wendy looked at her list. "We're building Mr Beasley's conservatory today," she told the team.

"Can we fix it?" said Scoop.

"Yes we can!" said the others.

"Er . . . yeah . . . I think so," said Lofty.

Bob and the team went to Mr Beasley's.

"Miaow!" said Pilchard. Bob had forgotten her breakfast!

Wendy marked out where the conservatory would go.

Scoop dug up the soil and Muck took it away. Scoop
unloaded bricks and Dizzy mixed concrete.

When all that was done, Bob and Wendy laid the bricks.

"This is thirsty work," said Bob. "Let's have a cup of tea and a sandwich."

But Bob couldn't find his sandwich box.

Wendy started to laugh. "Sorry, Bob," she said. She pointed to the wall. "I thought your sandwich box was a brick. Look, it's in the wall!"

Bob laughed, and took it out.

Pilchard went into Bobsville. She wanted to find Bob so he could give her some breakfast.

Pilchard saw a fish in Mrs Broadbent's basket. She nodded her head at it. **"Miaow!"**

Mrs Broadbent scratched Pilchard's ears! She thought that was what she wanted!

"Miaow!" said Pilchard, hungrily. She shook her head. That wasn't what she wanted at all!

Later on, Pilchard saw a bowl of dog food.

She sniffed it, then a loud, **"Woof!"** made her jump. She landed on the bowl and it rolled off down the street.

Pilchard ran after it – and found Bob!

When he saw the food bowl, Bob said, "Oh, sorry, Pilchard! I forgot all about your breakfast."

Lofty arrived. "I knew Pilchard wanted her breakfast," he said. "So I brought her bowl and a tin of cat food. But I forgot the tin opener!"

"Miaow!" said Pilchard. Oh, no!

"It doesn't matter," said Wendy. "Look, the can has a ring-pull."

"Breakfast, Pilchard!" said Bob.

"Miaow!" said Pilchard, happily. Food at last!

I like trying new things! When I heard about the Bobsville line dancing contest, I decided to take lessons and enter. Read about how I got my new name in . . .

Buffalo Bob

Bob and the team were hard at work in Farmer Pickles' field.

Lofty lifted hay bales from Travis' trailer. Bob nailed planks of wood together.

"What are you making?" asked Muck.

"It's the floor for the line dancing contest," said Scoop.

"What's line dancing?" asked Lofty.

"It's the kind of dancing cowboys do," said Bob. "We wear cowboy clothes and dance in lines. I'll show you."

Bob said, "Take your partner by the hand, step to the left and swing 'em round."

"You're good, Bob!" said Muck.

"Thanks," said Bob. "I had lessons. I'm dancing with Mavis from the post office."

When Bob went home to get ready, Scoop, Muck and Lofty tried a few steps. "One, two. One, two, three . . . "

Line dancing was fun!

Back in the yard, the phone rang. It was Mavis.

"Oh," said Bob. "Oh, well, never mind. Bye."

"Bad news?" asked Wendy.

Bob nodded. "Mavis has hurt her ankle. She can't dance tonight. I'll have to cancel our entry."

"Don't do that," said Wendy. "Dance with me!"

"Can you line dance?" asked Bob.

"No, but I can learn!" said Wendy – and she did.

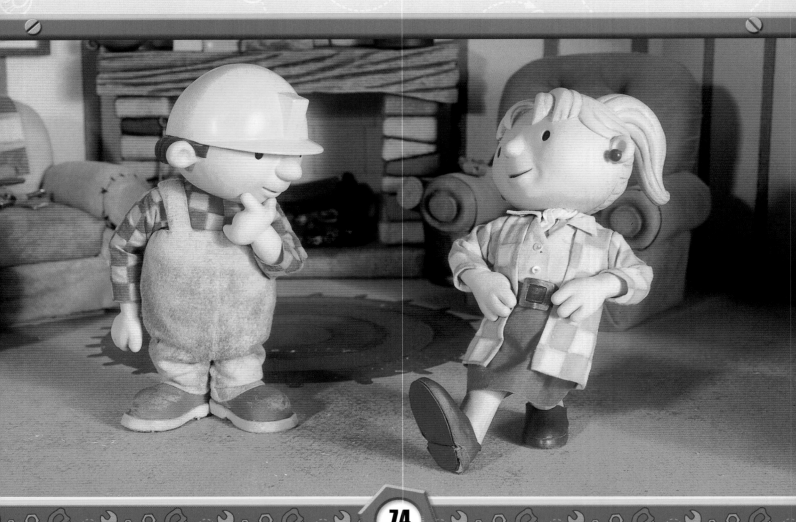

"Yee-hah!" said Bob. "You learn fast, Wendy. You're really good at this!"

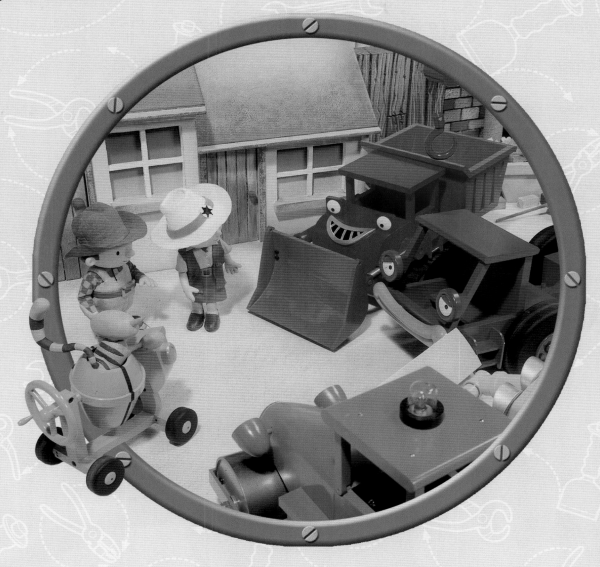

When Bob and Wendy were dressed and ready to leave, Scoop said, **"Can they win it?"**

"Yes they can!" said the others.

"I wish we could be in the contest," said Dizzy.

"Yeah," said Scoop. "Hey, I've got an idea!"

Soon line dancing music filled the yard!

Scoop, Muck and Lofty showed Roley and Dizzy some steps.

Then they all joined in.

Bob took Wendy home.

When Dizzy saw him she said, "Did you win?"

Bob held up a gold cup. "Yes!" he said.

"Three cheers for Bob and Wendy!"

said Scoop. "Hip, hip . . ."

"Hooray!" said the others.

Wendy heard them. She smiled happily

and said, **"Yee-hah!"**

Spud and Travis are good friends. But one day, when Spud tried to help Travis, things went badly wrong! Read about Spud's ride on a runaway trailer in . . .

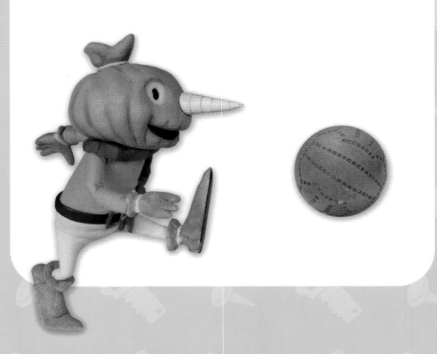

Trailer Travis

Wendy, Lofty and Dizzy were going to put up a new signpost.

"Can we build it?" said Wendy.

"Yes we can!" said Dizzy.

"Er . . . yeah . . . I think so," said Lofty.

Travis and Spud arrived to take some rubble to Farmer Pickles. Scoop put it into Travis' trailer.

Spud kicked Dizzy's football. It hit Roley, just missed Bird,

and bounced up on to the chimney.

"Oops!" said Spud, climbing up a ladder to get it.

Bird flew to the chimney and tapped the ball with his beak.

It rolled down the roof, and hit Spud on the head.

"Oof!" said Spud. "That hurt!"

"Nice shot, Bird!" said Scoop.

Bob and Muck built a new porch for Mrs Broadbent.

She put two apple pies into Muck's digger. "One for you, Bob, and one for Wendy," she said.

When Mrs Broadbent wasn't looking, Bob tapped one of the pies. It was rock-hard!

"Would you like some of my rock cakes as well?" asked Mrs Broadbent.

"Er . . . no thanks," said Bob.

Travis pulled the trailer full of rubble. It was hard work.

"I'll unhook your trailer so you can have a rest, Travis," said Spud.

"Nooooo!" said Scoop.

Too late! The trailer – and Spud – rolled away.
"Whoooa!" Spud shouted. "Heeelp!"

Bob was showing Wendy the pies when Spud appeared on the runaway trailer.

"Help!" he cried, waving his arms about. "Look out!"

"He's going to hit the signpost!" said Bob. "Quick, Wendy, take this pie. Ready? One, two, three . . . "

Bob and Wendy threw the pies in front of the trailer. It hit them, tipped forward – and stopped.

Spud flew through the air and landed, **bump!**

"Are you all right?" asked Bob.

"Yeah, course," said Spud. "I wasn't scared, not me! But I **am** hungry."

Bob showed him the squashed pies. "You can have these," he said.

Spud looked at the tyre marks on the pies. "Even I'm not **that** hungry!" he said. **"Yeuk!"**

Lofty is scared of all sorts of things – but especially squeaky mice. Read about the day when he heard lots of little squeaks and ran away in . . .

Bob's Boots

One morning, Bob came into the yard wearing a pair of new work boots.

Squeak, squeak!

Bob heard a sound, and stopped to listen.

When he stopped, so did the squeaks.

"Er . . . is it mice?" asked Lofty.

"No, don't worry, Lofty," said Wendy. "It's Bob's boots. They're squeaking because they're new."

At the farm Spud and Travis were arguing about the quickest way to Bob's yard.

"Turn left at the crossroads," said Spud.

"No, turn right," said Travis.

They asked Farmer Pickles to decide.

"The quickest way is as the crow flies," he said. "A straight line, like a bird flies. Now come on, Travis, there's work to do."

Spud turned to Bird. "I'm faster than any bird!" he said. "I'll race you to Bob's yard."

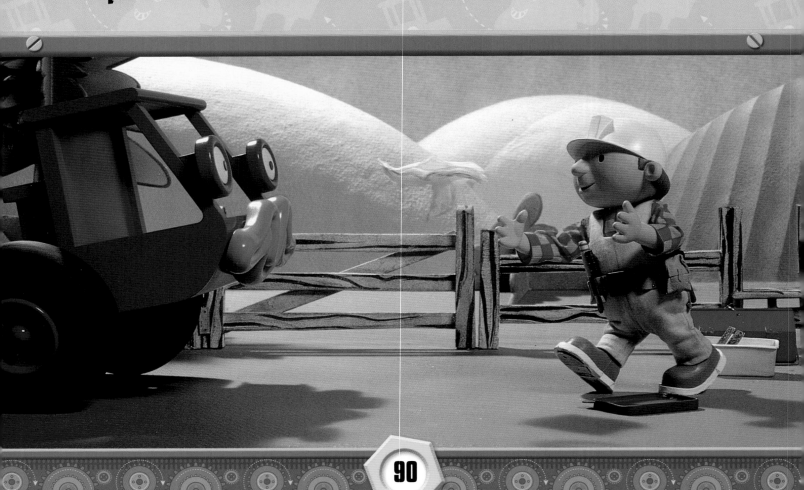

"**Toot!**" said Bird, and off he flew.

Lofty and Bob fitted a new gate at the farm. Then they stopped for lunch.

Bob opened his lunch box. A big gust of wind blew his paper napkin away.

Bob and Lofty chased after it. **Squeak, squeak, squeak!** went Bob's boots.

Spud was running along when he saw Bob's lunch box.
He stopped and looked inside.

"Yeuk!" said Spud. He didn't like Bob's cheese and chutney
sandwich. But his big cream bun looked yummy! "I'll save it,
and eat it later," he said.

"Toot!" said Bird, flying past him.

"Wait for me!" said Spud.

Bob caught his napkin. **Squeak, squeak, squeak!** went his boots.

Some little mice ran after him. **"Eek, eek, eek!"**

Bob was looking for his cream bun when Lofty saw the mice. "M-m-m-m-mice!" he said, running off. **"Arrrrgh!"**

Bob chased after him. **Squeak, squeak, squeak!** went his boots.

"Eek, eek, eek!" went the mice.

When Bob ran into the yard Lofty pointed to the mice.

"Look, Bob!" he said. "M-m-mice!"

"Eek, eek, eek!" went the mice.

"They like my squeaky boots!" said Bob.

When Spud arrived he saw the mice, too. **"Arrrgh!"** he said. "Mice! I'm off!"

"Have you had a busy day, Bob?" asked Wendy.

Bob laughed. "No, it's been as quiet as . . . a mouse!"

Muck loved the idea of having a sleep over at Farmer Pickles' farm one night. But that was before naughty Spud spoiled it by playing tricks on him. Read about it in . . .

Muck's Sleep Over

Muck helped Wendy build a new path at Farmer Pickles' farm.

"It's late. Why don't you sleep over at the farm tonight, Muck?" said Travis.

Muck liked that idea. "Yeah!" he said. "Can I Wendy, can I pleeeeese?"

"If you behave," said Wendy.

"I will!" said Muck.

When it got dark, Farmer Pickles said goodnight to Muck and Travis.

"It's fun here," said Muck. "But it is dark, isn't it? Very, very, very dark."

"It gets even darker," said Travis.

"Oh, d-d-d-d-does it?" said Muck.

"And quiet," said Travis. "It gets very, very, quiet."

"Oh d-d-d-d-dear," said Muck.

Spud was hiding. "It won't be quiet for long!" he said.

Travis closed his eyes and went to sleep. But Muck was too worried to even blink!

Snap! Spud broke a twig.

"Oh, w-w-w-w-what was that?" said Muck.

"Woo-woo!" Spud hooted like an owl.

"It's a m-m-monster!" cried Muck. "I don't like it! I'm going back to the yard!"

Bob, Lofty and Scoop were working late. They were fixing new lights in a tunnel.

Pilchard was with them. When she heard an owl hoot, she ran after it.

Bob ran after her – and bumped into Muck.

"What are you doing here?" asked Bob.

"It was d-d-dark," said Muck. "There were f-f-funny noises. I got s-s-scared. I was on my own."

"Well you're not on your own now," said Bob. "Let's find Pilchard."

At the farm, a real owl hooted.

Spud jumped, and landed on Pilchard's tail.

"Miaow!" said Pilchard.

"Hoot!" said the owl.

"Arrrrgh!" said Spud. "A miaowing-hooting monster!"

Bob found Pilchard and took her and Muck back to the

tunnel with him.

When the work was done, Bob took Muck back to the farm.

"But it's d-d-dark, and . . . " said Muck.

"It won't be," said Bob. He turned on the bright lights he had fixed up.

Muck closed his eyes.

Soon he was fast asleep, **zzzzzzzz!**

One Christmas, it snowed
hard in Bobsville. Dizzy got
covered in snow and gave
Spud a real scare! Read
about the snow monster
and Father Christmas'
special helper in . . .

Bob's White Christmas

It was Christmas Eve, and the machines were excited.

Scoop arrived with a big Christmas tree and Bob and Wendy decorated it.

"I wish it would snow!" said Dizzy.

"Me, too!" said Roley. "I love snow!"

Wendy looked at her watch. "You need to be at the school at four o'clock, Bob," she said.

"Oh, yes!" said Bob. "I said I'd be Father Christmas."

"Why can't Father Christmas go himself?" asked Lofty.

"He's . . . er . . . busy," said Bob. "He needs me to help him."

"You're one of his helpers!" said Scoop. "Wow!"

Just then a snowflake landed on Dizzy. "It's snowing!" she said. "Brilliant."

Muck and Scoop had a snow fight. Muck threw snow at Scoop. Scoop threw snow at Muck.

Then they both built a big snowman.

Wendy got a phone call from Farmer Pickles. "He's snowed in, Bob," she said. "He needs you and Scoop to dig him out."

"Can we dig it?" said Scoop.

"Yes we can!" said the others.

"Er . . . yeah . . . I suppose so," said Lofty.

When Bob had gone Wendy found he had left his phone behind. She asked Dizzy to take it to him.

But poor Dizzy got covered in snow. She was stuck!

Spud saw the big snow shape in his field. "Oo-er!" he said.

He ran off. "It's a s-s-snow monster! Heeeelp!"

Spud showed Bob the monster.

"Is that you, Bob?" said the monster.

"It knows you!" said Scoop.

"Of course I know him," said the monster. "It's me, Dizzy. I was bringing Bob's phone. I got stuck. I'm f-f-freezing!"

Bob rescued Dizzy and took her back to the yard. Then he put on his Father Christmas outfit and went off to the school.

Next morning, Wendy arrived at the yard. Her arms were full of presents.

"Happy Christmas, everyone!" she said.

"Happy Christmas!" said Muck. "Look, Father Christmas has left presents as well."

"And he didn't need any help from me," said Bob. "Happy Christmas, everyone!"

Wendy made plans to do some painting on her day off. But Scruffty had other ideas! Read about what Farmer Pickles' naughty puppy got up to in . . .

Watercolour **Wendy**

"Are you working with us today, Wendy?" Scoop asked one morning.

"No, it's my day off," said Wendy. "I'm going to do some painting at the farm."

"I'll carry your things for you," said Muck.

"Thanks," said Wendy. She put her things in Muck's digger and they set off.

Mr Bentley had a job for Bob. "I want you to lay these paving stones," he said. "They make a picture of the Bobsville coat of arms."

Bob went off with Mr Bentley. The machines got bored waiting for him.

"I know, let's do the coat of arms!" said Scoop.

But fitting the stones together was tricky. Their first try was wrong – and so was their second!

At the farm, Wendy told Muck he could stay.

Along came Scruffty. **"Ruff!"** he said. He barked, jumped around, and ran off with Wendy's phone!

Wendy ran after Scruffty. But when she caught up with him he didn't have her phone.

"He must have buried it!" said Wendy.

"Muck to the rescue!" said Muck.

Muck dug lots of holes, but he didn't find Wendy's phone.

Farmer Pickles had an idea. He threw a bone to Scruffty.

"Ruff!" said Scruffty. He ran off with it and put it in his

favourite hole.

Wendy's phone was in it!

"Thanks, Farmer Pickles," said Wendy. "Can I borrow

Scruffty for a while?"

"Yes," said Farmer Pickles.

When Bob came back, the stones were in the wrong places.

He pointed up to the clock tower. "Copy the picture. Look, there it is."

"Can we build it?" asked Scoop.

"Yes we can!" said Dizzy.

"Er . . . yeah . . . I think so," said Lofty.

This time, the team put the stones in the right places.

Later, back at the yard, Wendy showed Bob her painting.

It was a picture of Scruffty with her phone!

They heard a noise. **"Ruff!"**

"That's Scruffty's bark!" said Wendy. "But where is he?"

Scruffty jumped out of Muck's dumper.

"Ruff!" he barked. He wanted to see his picture!

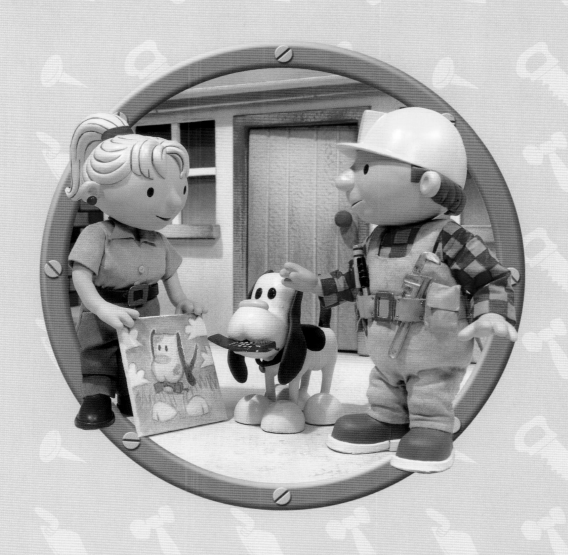

Roley thinks he's
a bit clumsy. But his big
rollers can be very useful.
Read about what happened
when he was working in
Mr Beasley's garden in . . .

Clumsy Roley

Bob went to fit a new kitchen for Mr Fothergill. He met Mr Fothergill's pet, Hamish.

"He's a parrot," said Mr Fothergill. "He talks a lot."

"Parrot!" said Hamish.

Bob opened his toolbox. "Screwdriver . . . " he said.

"Screwdriver!" squawked Hamish.

Wendy and the team went to make some decking for Mr Beasley.

Two squirrels jumped on to Lofty's cab. "Ooo-er . . . mice with bushy tails!" he said.

"No, they're squirrels!" said Wendy.

"I like them!" said Roley. He rolled around, singing, "I like to roll . . . "

But Roley rolled over Mr Beasley's watering can! He squashed it flat!

"Clumsy me!" said Roley.

Bob was working hard.

"Bob!" squawked Hamish in Mr Fothergill's voice.

"Did you call me?" Bob shouted.

"No," said Mr Fothergill.

Then Bob's phone rang, **brrrrrring!** "Hello," said Bob.

"Hello!" squawked Hamish.

Bob looked at Hamish. "You're playing tricks on me, aren't you?" he said.

Roley worked in Mr Beasley's garden. But he rolled into a tree! **Thud!** The squirrels' nest fell out!

"Oh, I'm so clumsy!" said Roley.

"Don't worry," said Wendy.

She made a new house for the squirrels.

Roley fixed it in place. This time he was extra careful.

"See, you're not clumsy!" said Wendy.

Soon the decking was finished. But on his way out, Roley rolled over Mr Beasley's flowers!

Mr Beasley didn't mind. "I put flowers in this book," he told Roley. "Then I press them flat. You're good at rolling. You can do it for me!" And Roley did!

Bob finished Mr Fothergill's new kitchen.

"We'll take the old units to the recycling centre," he told Wendy. "But they're very big."

"Roley can roll them flat for us," said Wendy.

"Clever Roley," said Bob. **"Can you squash them?"**

"Yes I can!" said Roley.

Farmer Pickles asked me to put up a new shed. He wanted Wendy to paint the farmhouse. Read about what happened when Spud decided to help in . . .

Scarecrow Dizzy

"What jobs do we have today?" Scoop asked.

"I'm painting Farmer Pickles' farmhouse," said Wendy.

"And I'm making a new shed for him," said Bob.

"Do you want to come?" Dizzy said to Pilchard. "You can ride in my mixer."

At the farm, Spud asked Wendy if he could help.

"You'll be extra careful, won't you?" Wendy asked him.

"Yes," said Spud. "Promise!"

Lofty wasn't sure, because Spud was always playing tricks.

Spud started painting, but he painted the ladder, not the wall! Then he gave Wendy a new tin of paint. But it was red, not white! Oh dear!

Bob made a cement base for the shed.

Pilchard jumped out of Dizzy's mixer when she saw some mice. She ran across the wet cement to catch them.

Dizzy tried to catch her, but she skidded in the wet cement!

Bob made the cement smooth again. Then he went to get the shed.

"You keep the birds off the cement, Dizzy," he said. "Like a scarecrow!"

Squawk the crow looked at the cement. "Please keep off it!" said Dizzy. "I'll give you a ride if you do!"

"Ark!" said Squawk.

Dizzy was very tired when Bob got back.

Bob's phone rang. "I need help," said Wendy. "Spud's better at scaring crows than painting!"

"I need help too," said Bob. "Dizzy's too tired to work. Let's swap helpers."

Dizzy went to help Wendy. "Look, there are bits of white wall and bits of red wall," said Wendy.

Dizzy knew what to do. "Let's mix the white and red paint, and paint the walls pink!"

When the farmhouse was finished, Wendy and Dizzy went to help Bob.

Pilchard was still chasing the mice.

They ran up Spud's trouser leg! "Get them off!" he cried.

Dizzy had another idea. "Let's paint the shed pink!" she said.

And that's how Farmer Pickles got a new **pink** shed as well!

Lofty helped Spud when he went skating on the frozen pond and the ice broke. Read about how we all helped some hungry ducks and a prickly family in . . .

Bob
and the
Big
Freeze

It was snowing in Bobsville.

"Yippee!" said Dizzy. "We can build snowmen and . . . "

"Work first," said Bob. "Some of Farmer Pickles' trees blew down. We're going to cut them up for firewood."

"And I'm taking Scoop to clear snow," said Wendy.

"Can we fix it?" asked Scoop.

"Yes we can!"

"Er . . . yeah . . . I think so," said Lofty.

While Bob cut up the trees, Dizzy and Scruffty went to the pond. It was covered in ice.

"Look at me!" said Spud. "I'm Spud the skater!"

Spud slid around, but he fell over, **thud!**

Then he fell over again – **thwump!**

Then – **crack!** – the ice started to break up!

"I'll get help!" said Dizzy.

Bob and Lofty went to the pond.

Lofty grabbed Spud's belt and lifted him off the ice.

Some ducks arrived. They looked very hungry.

"Can we help them?" asked Dizzy.

"You know, I think we can!" said Bob.

Scoop cleared the snow from a little tunnel. It was a place for hedgehogs to sleep, but now they were wide awake.

"Shall we put them back?" asked Scoop.

"No, we'll take them to the yard," said Wendy.

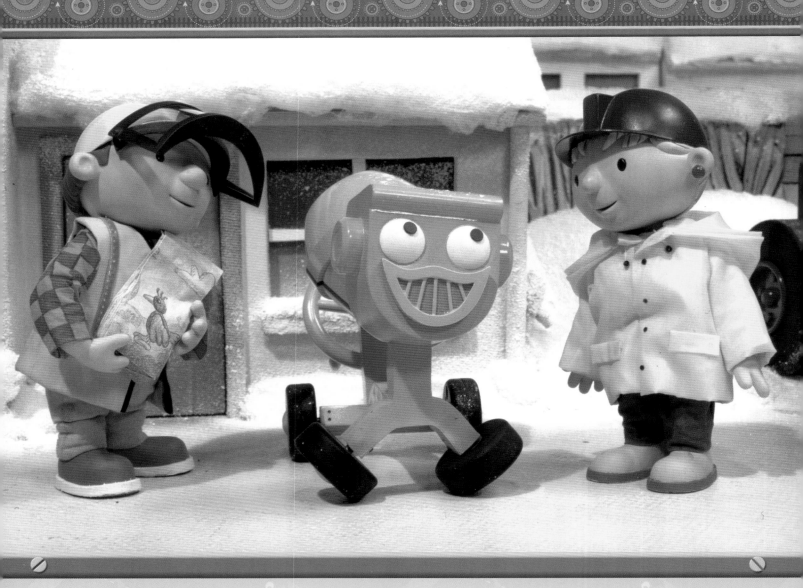

When they got there, Bob was putting seed in Dizzy's drum.

"It's for the ducks," he told them. "They're hungry. They need help."

Wendy told Bob about the hedgehogs. "They need help, too," she said. "They need somewhere to stay."

"Leave it to me!" said Bob.

Later, Bob showed the team a house he'd made for the hedgehogs. "I'll give them some of Pilchard's cat food then they can go back to sleep!"

The hedgehogs went inside.

"Do they like it, Bob?" said Roley.

"Yes they do!" said Bob.

Scruffty, the puppy, just loves chasing things! But when he chased two rabbits down a hole one day, he got himself stuck! Read about his scary adventure in . . .

Scruffty's Big Dig

One morning, Bob put cement into Dizzy's mixer.

"We're going to fix a wall at Mrs Broadbent's house,"
Bob told her.

Just then, Farmer Pickles arrived with Scruffty.

"Ruff!" said Scruffty. He went off to play.

Scruffty dug a big hole in Bob's garden. "He's like me!"
said Muck. "He loves digging!"

Scruffty looked at Bob. **"Ruff?"** he said. He wanted to go
with Bob.

"No, sorry, Scruffty," said Bob. "No dogs allowed on
a building site!"

The team went to Mrs Broadbent's house. "First we have
to take out the old bricks," said Wendy.

"But won't the wall fall down?" asked Dizzy.

"No," said Wendy. "We'll hold it up with metal props."

Bob put the props in place. Wendy took out the old bricks
and started to lay new ones.

Back on the farm, Scruffty chased two little rabbits. They ran into a rabbit hole to hide!

Scruffty dug and dug. But the soil gave way! He fell into a deep rabbit hole!

Muck was passing the field when he heard howls. He looked inside the hole. "Er, hello?" he said.

"Y-o-o-w-l!" howled Scruffty. **"Ooowww! Ow-ow-ow-ow-ow-oo-oo!"**

"Aargh!" said Muck. "A ghost!"

Muck took Bob and Lofty to the hole.

"Aa-ooooo!" howled Scruffty. **"Ruff! Ruff!"**

"It's Scruffty!" said Muck.

"Aa-ooooo!" said Scruffty.

Lofty used his hook to get Scruffty out of the hole.

"We'll fill in the hole," Bob said. **"Can we fill it?"**

"Ruff, ruff, ruff!" said Scruffty. Yes we can!

That night, Muck and Lofty told Roley what had happened.

"Lofty pulled Scruffty out," said Muck.

"But you found him," said Lofty.

Scruffty and Farmer Pickles arrived.

Scruffty gave Muck a bone.

"It's to say thank you," said Farmer Pickles.

"Lovely," said Muck. "But I don't like bones. You have it, Scruffty."

"Ruff!" said Scruffty. Thank you!

Roley just loves rock and roll music! Read about what happened when he helped make a garden pond for his favourite rock star, Lennie Lazenby, in . . .

Roley
and the
Rock
Star

Wendy, Muck and Lofty had a job to do on the nature trail.

"We're going to put signs up to show where the plants and animals are," said Wendy.

"And we're going to build a pond in Lennie Lazenby's garden," said Bob.

"Lennie Lazenby!" cried Roley. "Wow! He's the singer with The Lazers, my top band! Great!"

"Can we fix it?" said Scoop.

"Yes we can!" said the others.

"Er . . . yeah . . . I think so," said Lofty.

Wendy dug a hole for a sign and Lofty lifted it into place.

"Quack!" said a little duckling.

"What was that?" asked Wendy.

"It was a big . . . er . . . quacky thing!" said Lofty.

"A duck?" said Wendy.

"I don't know," said Lofty.

Lofty kept looking around.

"What are you looking for?" asked Muck.

"Quacky things!" said Lofty.

"Quack, quack!" said two ducklings.

"Ooooo-er!" said Lofty. "Scary!"

"The ducklings are more scared of you than you are of them, Lofty," said Wendy.

At Lennie Lazenby's house, Scoop dug a hole for the new pond.

Roley and Dizzy danced around to the pop music they could hear coming from the house.

"Rock and roll!" said Roley.

When the pond was finished Lennie came out to see it.

"Groovy!" he said. **"Real groovy!"**

Wendy, Muck and Lofty took the ducklings to their pond.

But it was just a muddy hole. There was no water.

"They need a new home," said Wendy.

She put the ducklings in Muck's scoop and took them to

Lennie's house. "Can we put them in your pond?" she asked.

"Sure!" said Lennie. "Ducks are . . . like . . . **groovy!**"

"Quack, quack!" said the ducklings.
"I think that means 'thank you'
in duck-talk," said Muck.
Lennie played his new song.
"Rock and roll!" said Roley.
"Quack, quack, quack!"
said the ducklings.

There's always something going on in Bobsville! Read about the special Fun Day when we all tried to win first prize in . . .

The Egg and Spoon Race

Bob and Wendy were going to run in the Bobsville Egg and Spoon race. They were practising.

Mr Sabatini was making a giant pizza for the winner!

"You've got to win!" said Dizzy. **"Yum!"**

"We'll try!" said Wendy. "But first we have to put in some new doors for Mr Sabatini."

"Can we fix it?" asked Scoop.

"Yes we can!" said the others.

All except Lofty. "Er . . . yeah . . . I think so," he said.

JJ was practising for the race as well.

When he went inside, Trix scooped up his egg. She turned round and round. "Trix can win it!" she said. But the egg rolled off her prong.

Muck arrived and caught it in his scoop.

"Nice catch!" said Bob.

Later, Spud arrived with some eggs for JJ.

Trix said, "Put one on my prong, Spud!"

She turned around but the egg flew off and broke, **splat!**

Another egg broke. Then another . . .

Soon all the eggs were broken!

"Erm, I'm off," said Spud. "Bye!"

When JJ saw the mess he said, "What happened?"

"Sorry," said Trix. "I was pretending to be in the race, but the eggs all broke."

At Mr Sabatini's, Wendy told Muck how to fix glass in the door frame. "We use sticky stuff called putty. It goes hard and holds the glass in place."

Spud heard what she said. "That's just what I need!"

Spud put some putty on his spoon. Then he pressed an egg on top. "I'm going to win that pizza!" he said.

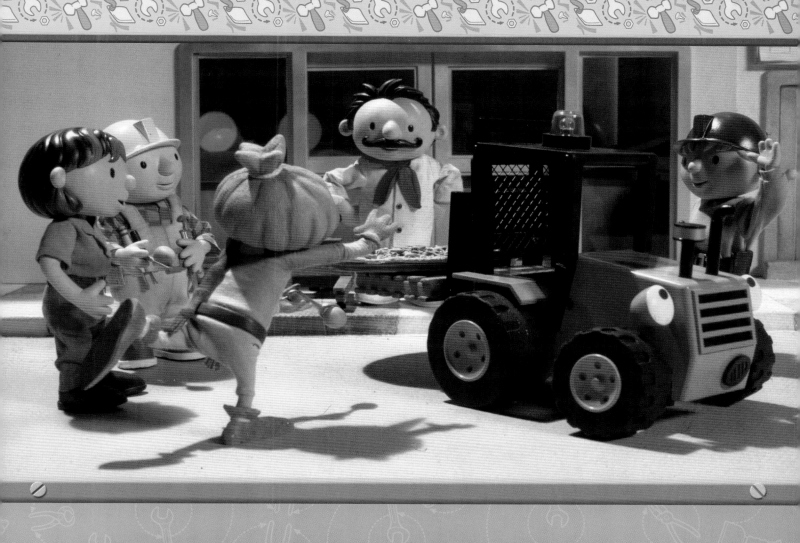

Spud did win the race! But when he waved his spoon around the egg was stuck to it!

"What's under your egg?" asked Mrs Percival.

"It's a bit of . . . er . . . sticky stuff to . . . " said Spud.

"That's cheating," said Mrs Percival. "Trix is the new winner of the Egg and Spoon race!"

Luckily, Mr Sabatini's pizza was so big that there was a slice for everyone – even Spud!

When JJ's little plane flew off on its own, Spud found it. Read about how he used it to scare Squawk, the crow, and where it ended up, in the story of . . .

Spud the Pilot

One morning, Bob said, "We're going to JJ's to get a new fireplace for Mrs Percival."

"Can we fix it?" said Scoop.

"Yes we can!" said the others.

All except Lofty. "Er . . . yeah . . . I think so," he said.

JJ's little plane buzzed over Bob's head. "It can do all sorts of things," said JJ. "Watch!"

Later on, JJ took his plane into the fields. It zoomed into the sky and looped the loop. But then it disappeared! JJ ran after it. "Come back!" he cried.

The plane landed near Spud. He picked it up. **"Neown!"** he said, running off. "Spud the pilot."

When JJ arrived, Spud was gone.

Spud found JJ's control box. He pressed a button. **Brrrrm!** went the plane. It flew up into the air, then dived!

Brrrrm! The plane flew at Squawk the crow.

"Squawk!" said Squawk.

Brrrrm! The plane dived at Squawk.

"Squawk!" said Squawk.

"He-he!" said Spud. "Scaring crows is easy with this little plane!"

Squawk flew off.

Spud ran after him, but he tripped up over a log.

"Ark, ark, ark!" laughed Squawk.

Spud pressed a button and the plane zoomed off.

"Come back!" yelled Spud.

The plane flew into town, to Mrs Percival's chimney.

The plane flew down into the chimney. Inside the house,

black soot and the plane burst out of the fireplace!

Bob and Mrs Percival took the plane outside.

"Is this your plane, Spud?" asked Mrs Percival.

"Er . . . no . . . I found it, but it flew off . . . "

Just then JJ arrived. "My plane!" he said.

"I'll fix it," said Bob. "But what about the mess?" He looked at Spud. "I think Mrs Percival needs some help cleaning up."

"Yeah," said Spud. "Oh . . . you mean me, Bob?"

Spud got busy cleaning up the mess. He pretended his feather duster was a plane!

"Neeeeeown!" said Spud. "Spud the pilot!"

Molly said she'd make the clothes for a fashion show. Dizzy wanted to be a model – and so did someone else! Find out who it was in the story of . . .

Molly's Fashion Show

Pam Goody bought a tin of yellow paint from JJ.

"It's for the new arts centre," she told Molly. "We need to raise more money to finish it."

"Why don't you have a fashion show?" said Molly. "I'll design the clothes."

"Great idea," said Pam. "Thanks!"

Molly said, "I'll get Bob on the job! He'll help."

Bob agreed to build a catwalk for the show.

"I'd like to be a model!" said Dizzy.

Lofty put a blue plastic sheet on her. "Wear this!" he said.

"Can we fix it?" said Scoop.

"Yes we can!" said the others.

All except Lofty. "Er . . . yeah . . . I think so," he said.

"A catwalk, eh?" said Spud. "Let's take a look, Pilchard."

"Miaow!" said Pilchard.

When they got to the arts centre, Bob was painting.

He tripped over Pilchard and yellow paint went everywhere!

"Pilchard wants to try the catwalk," Spud explained.

Bob laughed. "A catwalk's not for cats! It's for the models to walk along."

"Models, eh?" said Spud.

Back at JJ's yard, Molly was thinking of ideas for clothes.

"I need something special," she said. "But what?"

"Why don't you go and look at the catwalk?" said JJ. "That might give you some ideas."

Pilchard made yellow paw prints all over Dizzy's plastic sheet. She liked it.

"It looks great!" she said. "Make some more, Pilchard!"

Molly went to the arts centre to get some ideas for her clothes.

Dizzy was on the catwalk. She went over a bump and red paint splashed on Molly. That gave her an idea . . .

Molly made her clothes and took them to the arts centre.

Spud found bits of fabric that were left. He got busy, too!

Pam started the show. Bob and Wendy wore dungarees
with splashes of colour all over them! Dizzy wore the
plastic sheet with Pilchard's paw prints on it.

The show was over when Spud arrived. He wore an outfit made
of Molly's scraps.

It looked great, and everyone cheered and clapped. **"Hurray!"**

"Thank you, fans!" said Spud. "I'm Spud the supermodel!"

Skip thought it was
Scoop who had good ideas.
But when I was in danger,
it was Skip who came up
with a great idea to
help me. Read all about
it in . . .

Skip's Big Idea

One day, Mr Bentley came to the yard. "The Mayor wants somewhere special to hold the art show," he said. "Any ideas?"

"There's the Old Mill," said Scoop.

"What a great idea, Scoop!" said Mr Beasley.

Skip sighed. Why was it always Scoop who had good ideas?

"Can we fix it?" said Scoop.

"Yes we can!" said the others.

All except Lofty. "Er . . . yeah . . . I think so," he said.

There was lots of work to do on the Old Mill. There was

a big hole in the wall.

"I know, you can make it into a doorway!" said Skip.

"Yes," said Bob. "That's what I thought."

Muck put rubbish in Skip's skip.

He and Mr Beasley then took it to the tip.

They passed Mrs Broadbent's house on the way. She had put lots of old stuff outside.

"I've got an idea!" said Skip. "I'll take it to the tip for her. Oh, no, I can't. I'm doing a job for Bob."

At the Old Mill, Bob fixed a big tube to the scaffolding.

"It's a rubble chute," he told Roley. "We'll throw bricks down it into Skip's skip."

When Skip came back he had an idea. "Bob, you could make a chute to . . . "

Then he saw the chute. "Oh, you've already got one."

Skip went to the tip again.

On the way back, Mr Beasley got down to look at some ducks on the pond but Skip then forgot all about him!

Skip rushed back to the Old Mill and – **clang!** – he bumped straight into the scaffolding!

"**Whoa!**" said Bob as the poles bent and he nearly fell off. "Get me down!" Bob cried.

Skip had an idea! He went to Mrs Broadbent's house and came back with an old mattress.

"Climb into the chute, Bob!" he said. "You can slide down it and land on the mattress!"

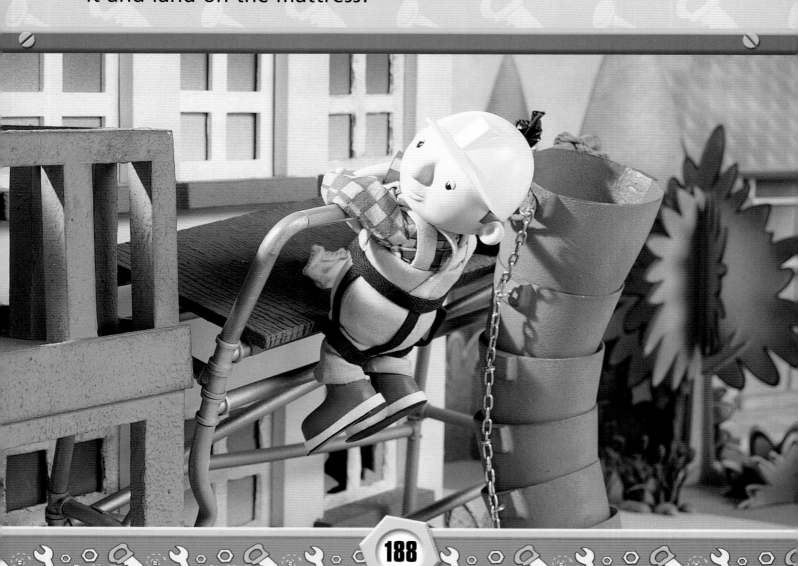

Bob got down safely. "Great idea, Skip!" he said.

Bob told Mr Bentley how hard the machines had worked.

"Especially Skip," he said. "He took lots of stuff to the

tip, and . . . "

"The tip!" cried Skip. "I forgot

all about Mrs Broadbent's stuff!"

He zoomed off again.

"Come back!" said Mr Beasley.

"Wait for me!"

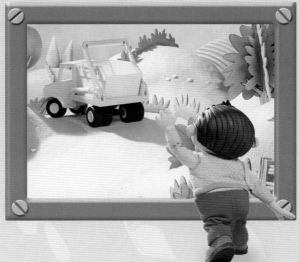

When Molly let Trix watch the otters with her, she was so loud and bright that they ran away. Read about how Scruffty and Muck helped Trix hide from them in . . .

Trix and the Otters

Wendy showed Muck a bucket of soapy water. "Do you want a wash?" she asked.

"No, I like being mucky," said Muck. "Like Scruffty. He's **really** dirty!"

"Ruff!" said Scruffty, happily.

"He's been rolling in the compost heap," said Farmer Pickles. "I need you to make a fence to keep him out."

"Can we fix it?" said Scoop.

"Yes we can!" said Muck.

"Er . . . yeah . . . I think so," said Lofty.

Trix took Molly to the pond to watch the animals.

"CAN I WATCH?" shouted Trix.

"No!" said Molly. "You scared the rabbits away!"

Trix went on to the farm.

Cheeky Scruffty flicked compost at her. Then he covered her in muddy paw prints.

Bob had to wipe the mess off Trix's shiny paint.

At the pond, Molly was quietly watching an otter and her cubs when Trix arrived.

"HELLO!" Trix shouted, making the startled otters run away.

"You scared them," said Molly. "If you want to watch the otters you have to be quiet, and hide."

The otters came back. But they saw Trix's bright purple paint and ran off again.

"THEY DON'T LIKE ME," said Trix, sadly.

At the farm, Scruffty covered Muck in compost!

When Muck met Trix she looked sad. "I want to watch the otters, but they keep running away," she said.

Muck went to see the otters. "They love mud, just like me!" he said.

"It's not fair!" said Trix. "Why doesn't Muck scare them?"

"They can't see him because he's mucky," said Molly. "He looks dull and brown."

"I've got an idea!" said Trix.

Trix went back to the farm. Scruffty and Muck slid around in the compost heap. Soon – **splish! splash! splosh!** – Trix was dirty and messy.

"Come on," said Trix. "Back to the pond!"

This time, the otters took no notice of Trix. "They **do** like me!" she said quietly. **"Brilliant!"**

When the Mayor of
Bobsville went on holiday,
she left her dog with Mr
Bentley. When Timmikins
got lost, can you guess
who found him?
Read about
the rescue
in . . .

Mr Bentley –
Dogsitter

Pilchard was hungry. She looked at Bob and said,
"Mrrrowrr!" but Bob took no notice.

Bob, Muck, Scoop and Dizzy went off to a job.
"Rrrrrrrowr!" said Pilchard, hungrily.

"Do you want some food?" asked Lofty.
"Miaow!" said Pilchard. She certainly did!

"Sorry, we don't have any," said Roley.

That made Pilchard angry. **"MIIIAAAAOW!"**

Bob was making a house into two flats.

Mr Bentley arrived with Timmikins, the Mayor's dog. "I'm looking after him while the Mayor is away," he said.

"Yip, yip!" said Timmikins. He jumped into Dizzy's mixer.

When Bob got him out he was very dusty.

"Take him to the yard," Bob told Mr Bentley. "Wendy will help you clean him up."

"Yip, yip!" said Timmikins. He liked the yard!

Mr Bentley went into the office to use the phone.

Wendy gave Pilchard a bowl of food. Then she went to get some soap and water.

Cheeky Timmikins gobbled up all Pilchard's food!

"Wrrrrroooaaar!" said Pilchard. She ran at Timmikins.

"Yip, yip!" snapped Timmikins. He chased Pilchard out of the yard.

When Wendy and Mr Bentley came back Pilchard and Timmikins were both gone!

At lunchtime, Bob closed the doors of the flats. He didn't see Timmikins run inside!

Mr Bentley and Wendy looked everywhere for Timmikins.

"I must find him," said Mr Bentley. "What will the Mayor say? We've got to find that dog!"

"Don't worry," said Bob. "We will."

Pilchard knew where Timmikins was! She pushed open the door of the flat and took him back to the yard.

When Timmikins saw Lofty, he ran at him. **"Yip, yip!"** he snapped.

"Oh, nooooo!" said Lofty. "Help! He's too noisy!"

When Mr Bentley arrived, Timmikins was very pleased to see him. He gave him a great big sticky lick!

"Well done, Pilchard!" said Wendy.

"Yes, you are a very clever cat, Pilchard," said Bob.

"Miaow!" said Pilchard.

"Yip, yip!" said Timmikins. He agreed!

When we built a new shop for Mr and Mrs Sabatini, there was no job for Roley. But that didn't stop him doing something really important for them! Read about it in . . .

Roley's Important Job

Bob was building a new shop for Mr and Mrs Sabatini.

"Is a lot-a work," said Mrs Sabatini.

"Yes, but we can do it," said Bob.

"Can we fix it?" said Scoop.

"Yes we can!" said the others.

All except Lofty. "Er . . . yeah . . . I think so," he said.

Poor Roley! There was nothing for him to do, so he went back to the yard.

Bird flew on to his cab. **"Toot-toot?"** he asked. What's wrong?

"I don't have a job to do," said Roley.

Just then Hamish the parrot flew into the yard.

"Toot!" said Bird.

"Toot!" said Hamish. He copies what people say.

"I know, I'll make up a song for the new shop," said Roley.

"It's the very finest deli," he sang.

"Finest deli!" squawked Hamish.

"Toot!" said Bird.

"No, no! Try again, birdies," said Roley. "The song has got
to be perfect."

"Better than anything on the telly," sang Roley.

"On the telly!"

"Toot!"

"No, that's still rubbish!" said Roley.

Bird looked at Hamish. Hamish looked at Bird. Then they both flew off!

When Roley found them, they were singing to Mr Sabatini's violin. "Sorry, birdies," he said. "It's just that the song needs – I know, a violin!"

When the shop was finished, Roley, Bird and Hamish sang their song. Mr Sabatini played his violin.

"It's the very finest deli," sang Roley.

"Finest deli!"

"Toot!"

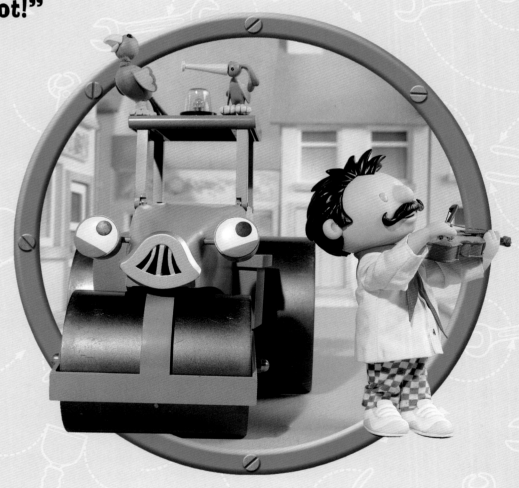

"Is-a the best-a song and the best-a shop!" said Mrs Sabatini. "You do-a a great-a job, Bob."

Bob smiled. "Thanks. We all had important jobs to do. But I think Roley's was the **most** important!"

"Thanks, Bob," said Roley.

Hamish had the last word, as usual.

"Thanks, Bob!" he squawked.

The famous goalkeeper David Dixon came to Bobsville to open a new fitness park we'd built. We took shots at him – even me! Read about who scored a great goal in . . .

Bob and the Goalie

One morning, Mr Dixon came to the yard. "We're going to have a new fitness park, Bob," he said. "We want you to build it! But that's not all! My brother, David Dixon, is going to open it for us!"

"You mean David Dixon the famous goalkeeper?" said Muck, excitedly.

"Wow!" said Lofty.

"Can we build it?" said Scoop.

"Yes we can!" said the others.

All except Lofty. "Er . . . yeah . . . I think so," he said.

Spud came to the yard.

Dizzy kicked her football to him. "Take a shot!" she said.

But Spud didn't kick the ball. "I'm, er, busy," he said, running off.

The team got to work. Muck brought the changing room. Lofty helped Bob fit it together. Scoop dug holes for the climbing frame.

"It's like a football goal!" said Dizzy. "Shoot, Bob!"

"Er, not today," said Bob.

Bob sat next to Spud to eat his lunch. "Why won't you play football?" he asked.

"I can't," said Spud. "I'm rubbish."

"Me too!" said Bob.

"Maybe we can have a game without the others," said Spud. "We'll use your orange as a ball!"

Spud tried to head the orange. It got stuck on the end of his parsnip nose!

Bob tried to kick the orange. He missed! He dived on it and squashed it flat!

"Huh!" said Spud. He threw the orange away.

David Dixon arrived. Wendy took him to the park.

"Take a shot," David told Dizzy. He saved it easily.

"You next, Bob," said David.

Bob kicked the ball. It hit the post and bounced out again!

"Your turn, Spud," said Dizzy.

Spud closed his eyes. He kicked as hard as he could.

The ball flew into the air . . . bounced off a bucket . . . hit a tree . . . bounced off the fence . . . and rolled towards the goal!

David saw it but he couldn't move. His foot was stuck in the bucket! He fell over . . . and the ball went into the goal!

"GOOAALL!" said Spud. "Spud the striker, that's me!"

One day, Muck dug up some things that were very, very old. An expert told us that they were important, as well as being old. Read about it in . . .

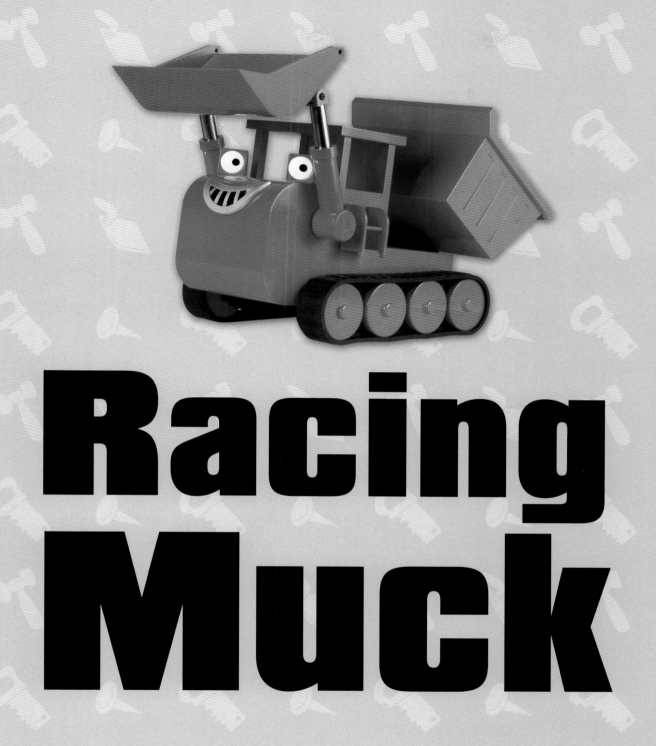

Racing Muck

Bob and the team were building a swimming pool!

Bob sent Muck to JJ's to pick up the tiles. "Be careful with them," he said.

At JJ's Trix put the tiles into Muck's dumper, and he set off. "Must-be-careful," he said. "Must-be-careful-with-the . . . "

Spud stopped Muck. "I need a lift," he said. "I'm late, I'll miss my dinner and . . . "

Muck took Spud to his field. "How do I get back?" he asked.

"Easy," said Spud. "Go left, right, then left again."

"Right," said Muck.

"No, left!" said Spud. "Look, just go straight across the field. Over there."

But the field was bumpy! **Bump-bump!** went Muck and **crack-crack!** went the tiles!

When Muck got to the site, all the tiles were broken!

"Oh, no!" said Muck. "Sorry, Bob."

"Don't worry," said Bob.

Trix brought more tiles. She showed Muck how to be careful with things. He soon got the hang of it.

Muck dug up some pieces of stone pottery. But they were all in pieces.

"Oh, no," said Muck. "I've broken them!"

"No," said Bob. "They're very old. They were broken a long time before you dug them up, Muck."

Mr Stephens came to look at the stones. He was an expert. He knew all about very old things.

"The stones are part of an old road," said Mr Stephens.

Muck helped Mr Stephens. He moved the soil so he could

see more stones.

"The road goes in a circle," said Mr Stephens. "And here's

an old wheel from a chariot! Muck, you've found a track

that was used for chariot races! We need to put up

a fence, and . . . "

"What about the swimming pool?" asked Muck.

"We'll put it somewhere else," said Bob.

When the work was done Bob put up a notice. It had Muck's picture on it.

"It's so people know who found the chariot track," said Bob.

"Let's try out the track!" said Mr Stephens.

Muck and the others had a race. I wonder who won?

One winter, Scoop wanted to build a snowman for the Bobsville Best Snowman Contest. When he couldn't, we fixed up a little surprise for him! Read all about it in . . .

Snowman Scoop

It was winter, and Bobsville was covered in a blanket of snow.

"I'm going to make my snowman for the Best Snowman Contest," said Scoop.

"Sorry," said Bob. "A water pipe has burst outside Mr Sabatini's. I need you to help fix it."

"No prob," said Scoop. **"Can we fix it?"**

"Yes we can!" said the others.

"Er . . . oof!" said Lofty, as Muck threw a snowball at him.

Bob put in the new pipe.

"Good-a work-a, Bob!" said Mr Sabatini. "Now let's-a finish-a my-a snowman."

Mr Sabatini gave his snowman olives for eyes. He made a moustache of chillies. Then a carrot nose!

At the farm, Spud saw some rabbits. "You look hungry," he said. "I haven't got any food for you." Then he thought of something. "Or have I?"

Later on, Bob and Scoop passed Mr Sabatini's shop.

He looked upset. "My-a snowman, 'ee is-a ruined," he said.

"Somebody steal-a 'ees nose!"

Someone had taken Mrs Potts' snowman's carrot nose, too!

"Just like Mr Sabatini's!" said Scoop.

Farmer Pickles rang Bob.

"We have to rescue Travis," said Bob. "He's stuck in the snow."

Scoop made a path with his snowplough. Muck pulled Travis free.

Scoop said, "There's another snowman with no nose! We can find the thief, Bob. Look, he's made footprints in the snow."

The footprints led to Spud. He had a bucket full of carrot noses!

"Why did you take them?" said Scoop.

"They're for the rabbits to eat," said Spud. "They're really hungry."

Scoop said he was going to help Spud.

"Scoop won't win the contest now," said Wendy.

"He might . . . " said Bob.

When Scoop got back, Mr Bentley was in the yard.

"I'm here to judge your snowman," said Mr Bentley.

"I didn't make one," said Scoop.

"But we did!" cried Bob.

He gave Scoop a carrot. "Here, give him his nose!"

Mr Bentley put a rosette on the snowman. "The best snowman – by a nose!"

JJ's forklift, Trix, likes to be helpful. But she sometimes gets in a muddle! Read about what happened when she tried to do two jobs at once in . . .

Trix's
Pumpkin Pie

JJ asked Trix to take a big bag of wood chippings to the school.

Bob and the team were making a climbing frame in the playground.

"What are the chippings for?" asked Trix.

"They go under the climbing frame," said Bob. "If the children fall off, they'll land on something soft."

Muck and Trix went to Farmer Pickles' farm for some poles. Farmer Pickles put some big pumpkins in Travis' trailer to sell them at the market. Two pumpkins were left.

"One's for a pumpkin pie for the Harvest Supper tonight," Farmer Pickles told them. "The other's a SURPRISE! Mrs Percival's going to bake the pie in Mr Sabatini's big oven. I need to take it to her . . ."

"We'll take the pumpkin **and** the poles!" said Trix.

She took the pumpkin to Mr Sabatini's.

Then she raced back to the school.

Trix moved the poles. Muck helped with the ropes. Lofty lifted up the roof.

The last job was to put down the wood chippings. But there weren't enough. "I'll get another bag!" said Trix.

Trix saw Mrs Percival outside Mr Sabatini's with the pumpkin pie. Trix said, "I'll take it to the farm for you."

On the way, she met Spud. "I'm taking the pie and the chippings," she said. "Which shall I do first?"

Spud grinned. "Take the chippings," he said. "I'll look after the pie for you!"

Trix met Wendy. "I'm in a muddle," said Trix. "I was taking the pie to the farm. But Bob needed the chippings. So I left the pie with Spud and . . . "

"Spud?" cried Wendy. "He'll eat it! Come on!"

They found Spud just in time!

"Thanks, Spud!" said Trix. She took the pie to the farm.

That night, Farmer Pickles showed everyone his surprise pumpkin. It had a face, with lights inside!

Mrs Percival cut the pumpkin pie. She gave the first big piece to – Spud!

"You deserve it. There wouldn't **be** any pie if you hadn't looked after it," said Trix.

Spud took a big bite. **Munch!** "Yeah," he said. "Can I have another piece, please?"

My cat, Pilchard, can be naughty sometimes! When she followed us to Mr Ellis' cottage, I was cross with her. But she made herself useful in the end! Find out what happened in . . .

Pilchard and the Field Mice

Bob and the team were going to fix a new beam in Mr Ellis' cottage.

"Miaow?" said Pilchard. She wanted to go with them.

Bob jumped on to Muck. "No, you can't come," he said.

"Can we fix it?" said Scoop.

"Yes we can!"

"Er . . . yeah . . . I think so," said Lofty.

Pilchard jumped into Muck's dumper! Bob didn't see her.

Muck went to JJ's yard.

Trix put the things Bob needed into Muck's dumper.

Pilchard jumped out. **"Miaow!"**

"Bad cat!" said Bob. He took her back to the yard. But
naughty Pilchard followed him back to Mr Ellis' house!

Bob worked on Mr Ellis' beam. He didn't see three little field mice under his bench.

But Pilchard did!

"Miaow!" she said.

"What are you doing here?" said Bob. He put her in the house.

"Yeowl!" said Pilchard.

She didn't like that!

The field mice ran in and hid under the sofa.

Pilchard scratched it.

"Bad cat!" said Bob, putting her outside.

When Wendy opened the door Pilchard ran in.

"Eek, eek!" said the field mice as they ran out!

"So that's what's been bothering Pilchard!" said Bob.

The field mice jumped into Muck's shovel.

"You can take them to the farm later," said Bob.

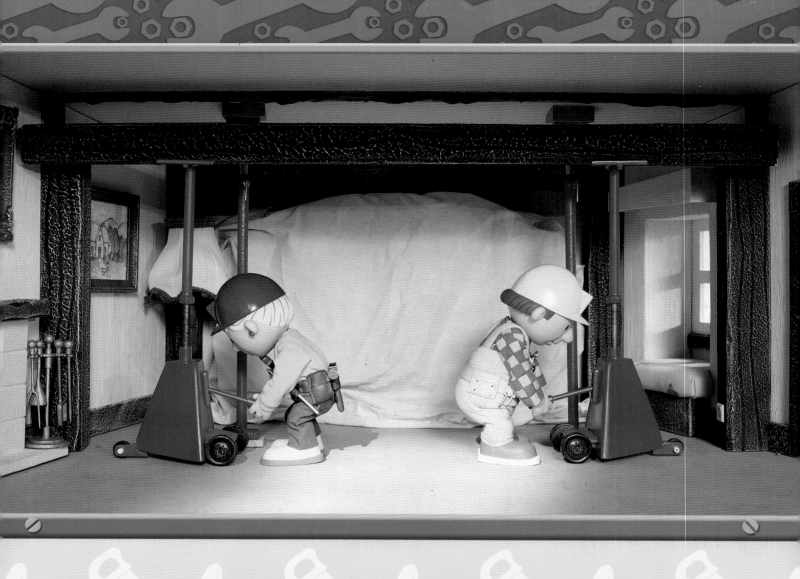

Bob and Wendy fitted the new beam. Mr Ellis was very pleased with it.

He was very pleased with Pilchard, too. "She got rid of the field mice for me," he told Bob. "I got her this clockwork mouse as a little thank you present."

Mr Ellis wound up the clockwork mouse and put it on the ground.

It **whizzed, whirred** – then raced off.

Pilchard was right behind it! **"Yeee-owl!"** she said. This was better than chasing **real** mice!

Bob laughed. "Thanks, Mr Ellis," he said. "You've just made Pilchard a very happy cat!"

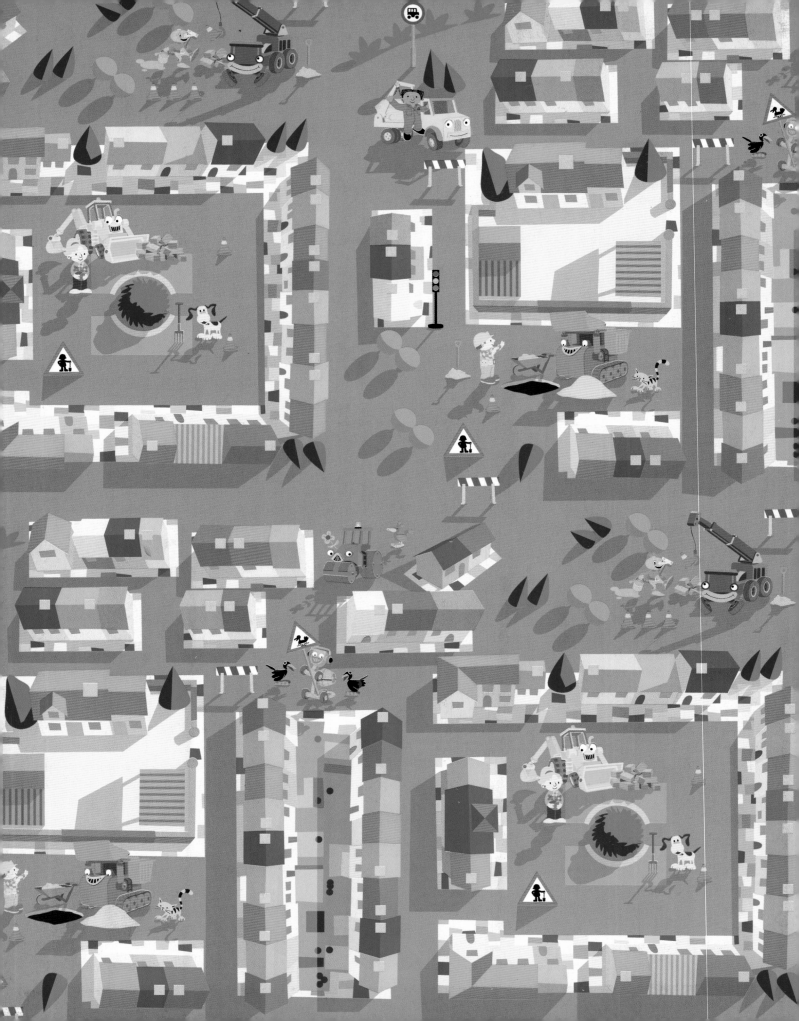